The Young Reader's Shakespeare
JULIUS CAESAR

A Retelling by ADAM McKEOWN

Illustrated by JANET HAMLIN

STERLING

New York / London
www.sterlingpublishing.com/kids

STERLING and the distinctive Sterling logo are
registered trademarks of Sterling Publishing Co., Inc

Library of Congress Cataloging-in-Publication Data

McKeown, Adam (Adam N.)
    Julius Caesar / a retelling by Adam McKeown ; illustrated by Janet Hamlin.
        p. cm. -- (The young reader's Shakespeare)
    Includes index.
    ISBN-13: 978-1-4027-3579-0
    ISBN-10: 1-4027-3579-0
    1. Caesar, Julius--Assassination--Juvenile fiction. 2. Brutus, Marcus Junius, 85?-42 B.C.--Juvenile
fiction. 3. Rome--History--Civil War, 43-31 B.C.--Juvenile fiction. 4. Conspiracies--Juvenile fiction. 5. Assassins--Juvenile fiction. I. Hamlin, Janet, ill. II. Shakespeare, William, 1564-1616.
Julius Caesar. III. Title.

        PR2878.J7M38 2008
          813'.6--dc21

                        2007030733

        2 4 6 8 10 9 7 5 3 1

Published by Sterling Publishing Co., Inc.
387 Park Avenue South, New York, NY 10016
© 2008 by Adam McKeown
Illustrations © 2008 by Janet Hamlin
Distributed in Canada by Sterling Publishing
c/o Canadian Manda Group, 165 Dufferin Street
Toronto, Ontario, Canada M6K 3H6
Distributed in the United Kingdom by GMC Distribution Services
Castle Place, 166 High Street, Lewes, East Sussex, England BN7 1XU
Distributed in Australia by Capricorn Link (Australia) Pty. Ltd.
P.O. Box 704, Windsor, NSW 2756, Australia

Printed in China

Sterling ISBN-13: 978-1-4027-3579-0
        ISBN-10: 1-4027-3579-0

For information about custom editions, special sales, premium and
corporate purchases, please contact Sterling Special Sales
Department at 800-805-5489 or specialsales@sterlingpub.com.

CONTENTS

ABOUT SHAKESPEARE AND *JULIUS CAESAR*

Julius Caesar is one of William Shakespeare's most popular plays—so popular that many people quote it without even realizing they are doing so. Phrases like "the dogs of war," "it's Greek to me," and "the evil that men do" are now part of ordinary English, a fact that says more about the importance of the story you are about to read than any introduction could.

For all its popularity, however, *Julius Caesar* is one of the most challenging plays Shakespeare ever wrote. On its surface it is another play that deals with one of Shakespeare's favorite issues: political struggle. Unlike *Hamlet*, *Macbeth*, *King Lear*, or *Henry IV*, however—all of which deal with political struggles of different kinds—*Julius Caesar* makes it very hard to tell which side of the struggle is right and which side is wrong. As you read this book, you will see that the story revolves around two Roman senators, Brutus and Marc Antony. Both are good and bad. Both seem at times reasonable and patriotic and at other times violent and selfish. Both form allegiances with other Romans who are also good and bad. Both are willing to risk plunging their country into chaos in order to save it. If, as you read along, you find it difficult to decide whose side you are on, don't worry that you aren't reading carefully enough. The play does not give you an easy answer, and that is part of the fun of *Julius Caesar*.

The title of the play tells us that Shakespeare probably intended us to have mixed feelings about it. Playwrights of Shakespeare's era were encouraged to write tragedies according to a tradition established by the ancient Greeks. For the Greeks, a tragedy was supposed to have a "tragic hero." The tragic hero is the most important character in the play, an admirable but also flawed person whose actions bring about his or her own destruction in the final act. If you were going to the theater in 1599 to see a brand new play called *The Tragedy of Julius Caesar*, you would be very surprised to learn that Julius Caesar has relatively few lines and does not even make it to the end of the play. You might have left the theater back then—as audiences still do—trying to figure out who the tragic hero is supposed to be. Brutus is the obvious choice, but others see Cassius or even Marc Antony as tragically heroic.

Why Shakespeare wanted to leave his audiences guessing about the hero of *Julius Caesar* is a mystery we will never solve completely. When Shakespeare died in 1616, he did not leave behind any personal memoirs, and all we have to go on is the play itself. Does the play give an answer? Maybe. Put yourself in the story for a moment. It is 44 B.C. Rome is a republic, like the United States, governed by the consent of the people. Julius Caesar is a military hero loved by the Roman people—so much so that they want to make him their king. You are a senator who believes that in a republic the wishes of the people should be honored, but you also know that if the people get this one wish they will never have a voice in government again. Do you oppose the will of the people today in order to ensure they have a voice in government tomorrow? Do you have that right? Is it your responsibility? What if you have to form partnerships with sinister people to accomplish something good? What if you have to kill? The world of *Julius Caesar* is a world of very complicated questions for which simple answers will not do. Neither, perhaps, will simple definitions like "hero."

Of course, the complex world of *Julius Caesar*—a world without clearly defined heroes and villains—is also our world. *Julius Caesar*, more perhaps than any other play Shakespeare wrote, seems to reach out to us from the past and remind us that today's difficult political decisions are not new. At one point in the play—after the death of Caesar—Cassius says, "How many ages hence shall this our lofty scene be acted over in states unborn and accents yet unknown?" The choices our leaders must make and the choices we must make with regard to our leaders are never simple, and often thoughtful decisions have unwanted and even disastrous consequences. If *Julius Caesar* does not make it easier to know how to cope with the political uncertainty of the world we live in, it at least reminds us that we are not alone, that other states have faced challenges long before ours was ever born, and that somehow we have always managed to regroup and continue on.

Chapter One

MURELLUS AND FLAVIUS heard the shouting all the way from
the Capitol. It was the sound of thousands of men coming closer,
moving as one body, crying out in one voice.

Trouble had been brewing since Rome's great general, Julius Caesar, came
home from his wars. The people had been reveling nonstop, growing each day
more unruly. They hailed Caesar as a protector who kept them safe from the
barbarians who dwelled beyond the mountains in the north, and they loved him
as a champion who spread the glory of their city to the farthest corners of the
world. But lately things had changed. Now there was talk of making Caesar
king.

"If the people have their way it will mean the end of the Republic," said
Murellus, panting as he ran, "the end of democracy in Rome and all we hold
dear."

"Especially our jobs," said Flavius.

Flavius and Murellus were tribunes, common men appointed to speak on
behalf of the common people to the Senate. They were supposed to make sure
the Senate paid attention to their wishes, but the people were often fickle in
their demands. They could love something one minute and hate it the next.
Worse, they could want something for the moment that would be bad for them
in the long run. Often Flavius and Murellus found themselves trying to convince the people of what they should want rather than listening to what they did
want. Sometimes it felt like they worked for the Senate and not the people.
Now was one of those times.

In the market square, the people were climbing up Caesar's statue, draping it with garlands and scarves. "Caesar! Caesar!" they chanted. "Long live Caesar!"

Flavius pushed through the agitated crowd and climbed the base of the statue. "Is this a holiday?" he shouted to the distracted multitude, who seemed not to hear. "I said, *is this a holiday!*"

"Look," said one man, as the crowd settled down. He was squat and rough, as if he were accustomed to hard work, but today he wore his best white robe. "It's the tribunes, come to tell us we shouldn't be happy."

Everyone laughed and waited to hear what Flavius would say next.

"What do you mean by going about in your best clothing, chanting and singing? This is a work day. Don't you have anything better to do?" said Flavius.

"Leave us be," the man shouted back. "What's wrong with celebrating Caesar's victories?"

Murellus, who stood among the people, confronted the man. For Murellus, the best way to handle a disorderly crowd was to speak without fear. People were easily intimidated by strength. "What is your profession?" he said to the man.

"I am a cobbler," the man answered.

"So why aren't you mending shoes? Where are your hammer and your apron?"

"You'd better mind your manners," he said, "or I'll show you my hammer up close."

A murmur went up and the crowd pressed forward around Murellus.

Flavius saw that the mob was about to turn violent. The people's love for Caesar was about to transform into hatred for anyone who contradicted them. "Romans," Flavius said, pointing across the square. "Do you see that statue? The statue of Pompey?"

"What's Pompey got to do with this?" said the cobbler.

"Caesar is not the first to win victories for Rome," said Flavius. "Pompey fought to preserve the greatness of this city and the freedom you enjoy as citizens of this Republic, but it seems you have forgotten him." Flavius tried to meet as many eyes as he could. "If you make Caesar a king, you spit on the memory of Pompey and all those heroes who have preserved democracy for us. Does freedom and democracy mean so little to you that you would throw it away to honor Caesar?"

The people fell silent.

Murellus circulated through the crowd. "You blocks, you stones, you worse than senseless things. Such ingratitude. Such foolish and shortsighted ingratitude."

Flavius stepped down and put his hand on Murellus' shoulder, as if to calm him down. "Go," he said to the crowd. "Take off your holiday clothes. Go to the Tiber and kneel. Stare at your reflection in its waters. Think about the freedom Rome, not Caesar, has given you. Think of all the great men like Pompey who gave you that freedom. Think no more about kings."

The tension in the crowd slackened as Flavius spoke, and slowly the knot of people began to untie itself.

"Why can't they see that having a king would mean the end of their freedom?" said Flavius as the people trudged away.

"Because they are idle and senseless," said Murellus, "and they don't understand what it means to be free."

The cobbler, who was the last to leave, turned. "And you don't understand the people you serve," he said.

Chapter Two

J ULIUS CAESAR, rugged and vigorous, walked down the marble halls of the Senate like the guest of honor at a party. He paid little mind to the people who flocked around him. To Caesar the world was full of little people who needed to be pitied, not honored. "Where is my wife?" he called. "Where is Calpurnia?"

"Caesar speaks!" said Marc Antony, who had been Caesar's most loyal follower for years. "Someone go get Calpurnia."

Quickly two attendants ran off.

"When Caesar says 'do this' it is performed," said Marc Antony, bowing.

When Caesar says "do this" it is performed. How sickening, thought Cassius, who was leaning against the wall and watching the spectacle of devotion with disdain. *What a pompous fool is Caesar. Look how that old slouch Marc Antony fawns on him to feather his own nest.*

Caesar pulled Marc Antony to him. "Who is that man?"

Marc Antony followed Caesar's eyes. "That is Cassius, a noble Roman."

"I don't like him," said Caesar. "He has a lean and hungry look. He thinks too much, I can tell. He is not like you, Antony. Yes, I can tell. Such men are dangerous."

"Fear him not, Caesar," said Marc Antony.

"I can't hear in that ear," said Caesar. "Come around this side and tell me truly what you think of him."

From the crowd came an old and creaky voice. "Let me through!"

Now this should be interesting, thought Cassius, as a blind man in ragged clothes clawed his way through the Senate.

"Where is Caesar?!" the blind man said.

Marc Antony tried to keep the old man away. "A beggar. Pay no mind to him, my lord."

"I am no beggar," said the man. "Where is Caesar?"

"Let him come," said Caesar. "I fear no one."

The blind man pointed his skinny finger in the direction of Caesar's voice. "Beware the ides of March," he said.

"What did he say?" Caesar turned his good ear to the man.

"A fortune-teller bids you to beware the ides of March," said Cassius from across the room, loudly enough to be heard by all.

Caesar stared at Cassius and then at the fortune-teller. "You are a dreamer, and I fear nothing." Caesar straightened. "Where is my wife!?"

Two more of Caesar's attendants ran off to find Calpurnia. Marc Antony hung by the great man's side as he marched down the hall.

Cassius watched them go. *Caesar is a disease*, he thought. *But there is a cure.*

Chapter Three

From the balcony of his villa, Brutus, Rome's most influential senator, looked down on the streets of Rome and listened to the noise of the crowd. The people were once again flooding the streets and chanting Caesar's name. But they were angry this time. They still wanted Caesar as their king, but now saw the Roman Republic as an enemy. The two tribunes, Flavius and Murellus, had been attacked when they tried once more to intervene. Whether they were alive or not, Brutus did not know.

A king, thought Brutus. *Why should free people want a king? But, then again, isn't standing in the way of what the people want, even for the good of Rome, a form of tyranny?*

Brutus listened as the chants became louder. The people were going to have their king or destroy Rome in the process.

At that moment Cassius came up quietly to Brutus' side. "You aren't down among the people, sharing in Caesar's latest triumph?"

"I am not in a festive mood."

Another shout went up.

"I do fear the people will choose Caesar for their king," said Brutus.

"Ah, do you fear it?" Cassius turned to Brutus, his bony face contracting into a wolfish grin. "Then may I assume you would prevent it?"

"I would, Cassius, and yet he is a hero, and the people love him."

"Are not you, Brutus, a hero and do they not love you? Would they not just as soon make Brutus their king?"

Brutus made no reaction to Cassius' words, as if he had expected them or, indeed, had the same thoughts himself.

"Look," continued Cassius, "I was born as free as Caesar, and so were you. We both endure the winter's cold as well as he. So why has he become a god and not you?"

Another shout came from the streets. "I am not sure it is as bad as all that," said Brutus.

"Heh," snorted Cassius, "he walks across the narrow world like a Colossus, and we petty men walk under his legs searching in the dust for our miserable graves." Cassius leaned in and spoke in a whisper. "But it does not have to be that way. We have the power to change things. Brutus, you do not see yourself as other men see you."

Brutus cut Cassius off. "I know what you are getting at. I confess the idea has also occurred to me. But no more for now."

A crash arose from the Roman streets, followed by shouting. Something had been broken. Was it the statue of someone who rivaled Caesar's greatness? The house of someone who opposed the people?

"Fair enough," said Cassius. "But tomorrow Caesar is supposed to go to the Senate, and I am sure he will be offered a crown."

"I will think on what you have said."

"Good. Then think on this too: when did the streets of this great city become so narrow they can hold only one man?"

Chapter Four

That evening a violent storm blew in from the sea. Rain swept down the Roman streets, and the Tiber swelled in its banks. Lighting tore across the sky, making strange and, some said, unnatural shapes.

Two hooded men came together in a secluded alley, sheltered from the winds.

"I fear the heavens read our minds and are scolding us." It was Casca, a senator who once had been Caesar's most loyal supporter, but who had grown increasingly fearful of his power. He looked around uneasily.

"Scolding us?" came the low voice of Cassius from beneath his hood. "I say the heavens are raging against the monster that Rome is creating."

Lightning erupted in the sky. Casca could swear he saw in the flash the faces of dead men. "You mean the crowning of Caesar, I suppose?"

"Think of it," said Cassius. "A *king* in Rome. A tyrant. The only reason he has become such a wolf is that he knows the Roman people are sheep."

A clap of thunder rang loudly, followed by the groaning of the wind.

"Someone approaches!" said Casca.

"It's Cinna," said Cassius. "I told him to meet us."

"What news?" said Cinna, a senator who, like the others, feared what Caesar had become.

"Tomorrow the people will make Caesar king," said Casca.

"And we meet tonight to resolve how to prevent that," said Cassius.

The men listened silently to the wind and the rain as the meaning of Cassius' words sank in. They were dangerous words.

"Do we have enough men on our side?" said Cinna, at last.

"The two of us," said Cassius. "Metellus, Decius, and Trebonius, as well."

"What about Cicero?" said Cinna. "Has anyone spoken to Cicero? His gray hairs will give our plan an air of dignity."

"I have," said Casca.

"What did he say?"

"He spoke Greek."

"Greek?"

"Well," said Casca, "it was Greek to me. I hinted at our plans and he replied with some long response I couldn't understand. Forget about that old man. He can't help us."

"What about Brutus?" said Cinna.

Thunder boiled in the sky. Nobody spoke.

"Are you telling me Brutus is not with us?" said Cinna. "Without him we have no chance!"

Brutus was everything Roman citizens believed a senator should be. He was tall and handsome, soft-spoken but firm. His every concern seemed to be for Rome and never himself. Their plan needed his support.

"Tonight," said Cassius, "we will gain Brutus' allegiance. That is why I have called you here. Brutus is a noble Roman but also a proud man, though he would never admit to it. I know in my heart he would rid Rome of Caesar, but only if he could believe it was best for Rome."

"So how shall we convince him?" said Cinna.

"Take these notes," said Cassius, handing Cinna and Casca letters carefully wrapped in wax paper and attached to stones. "Take them and throw them into Brutus' windows. Make it seem as if the people of Rome are coming to him for help."

In the flash of lightning, Casca and Cinna could see the rows of teeth in Cassius' savage grin.

"With Brutus on our side we can't fail," said Cassius.

Chapter Five

B RUTUS paced in his study, staring through his window at the strange shapes that appeared in the heavens. What time it was he could not guess, for there were no stars visible through the veil of storm.

His thoughts had been swirling since he had spoken with Cassius. He believed himself a true and loyal servant of Rome, and the democratic Rome he loved had no place for kings. But what was the alternative?

In the shadows outside his window Brutus saw what looked like a wild beast dragging its bulk through the streets. A lioness.

Everything was wrong, he thought as he watched the animal disappear into an alley. *The sky weeps. Beasts roam the streets. Tomorrow we shall have a king.*

A king. He pondered the strange shapes beyond his window and thought about what Cassius had said. *If killing one man would save a whole nation,* he thought, *wouldn't it be right to kill him? Even if he personally did nothing to deserve death?*

"What is on your mind, Brutus?" came a woman's voice. It was Portia, Brutus' wife and his best friend.

"It is too cold a night for you to be out of bed," Brutus said.

"I heard a lioness bellow as if she were giving birth in the streets," said Portia. "The night is troubled and confused. *You* are troubled and confused." She came closer. "For days you have slept little and eaten less. When I ask you what the matter is, you say nothing. Can you not tell me the cause of your grief?"

"I have not been feeling well," Brutus said uneasily.

"Have I given you some cause to believe that I cannot be trusted with your secrets, whatever they may be? Have I ever let you down?" Portia put her hand on the back of Brutus' neck.

As Brutus stood there trying to decide whether or not to talk to Portia about Caesar a rock flew in from the south window. Attached to it was a letter.

"What's this?" said Portia. She opened the note. "It says, *Brutus, you sleep. Awake and see yourself!* What does this mean?"

Brutus read the note, puzzled. "I wonder who threw it in here."

Just then another note flew in, and then another.

"This one says, 'Should Rome have a king?'" read Portia. "And this one, 'Speak, Strike, Redress!' Brutus, these are very serious words."

"Let me see those," said Brutus.

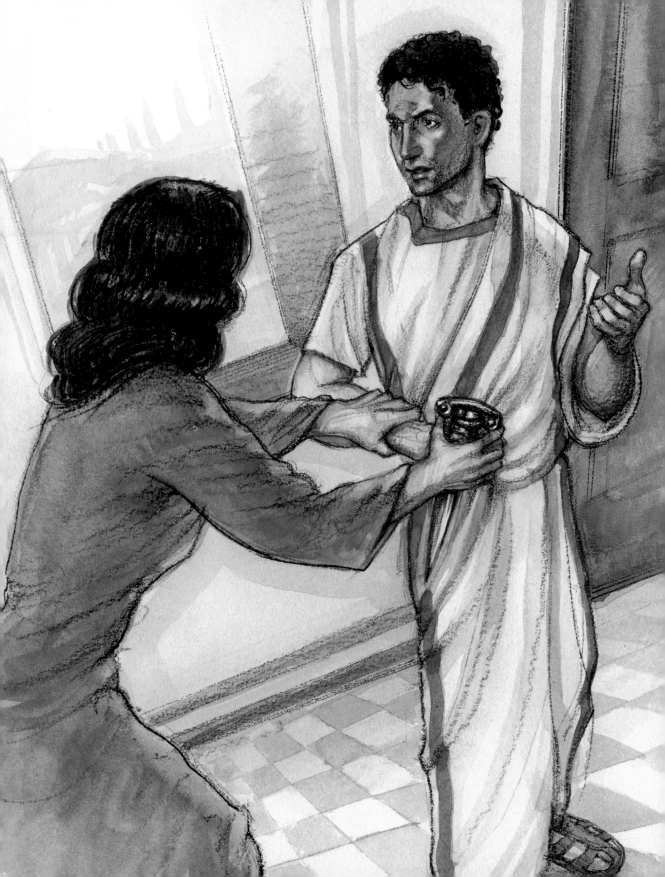

Brutus read the crude handwriting over and over. Were the people of Rome asking him to rise up in their defense? He felt suddenly enraged at Caesar and his followers. They had stirred Rome to such a state of frenzy that the only safe way of protesting was to throw notes through windows in the dead of night. He also felt something else. Pride. The Roman people were coming to him for help. They looked to him to save Rome.

"Husband," said Portia, "these messages speak of something dangerous, and yet—" She broke off.

"And yet?" said Brutus.

"And yet all of us who love the Republic are worried about the growing power of Caesar."

"I would not involve my wife in these matters."

"Your wife?" said Portia.

"Yes," said Brutus, "my wife."

Portia reached for the dagger in Brutus' belt. "I love Rome as much as any man, and my faith is just as hard. So is my courage." She plunged the dagger into her thigh. She did not so much as flinch. "If I can bear that pain I can bear your secrets, as I always have."

"Merciful gods!" said Brutus, pulling the blade out of Portia's thigh and using his own coat to stop the blood. "I would not involve you because I love you and wish to protect you!"

"You are my husband, and I love you. I am a Roman and I love this city. That is why I want to help, no matter the cause or the risk."

"My lord! My lord!" Brutus' servant ran into the room, still in his night-clothes. "There are men at the door. Cassius and others. They wish to speak with you. They say it is urgent."

Portia looked into her husband's eyes. She knew why the men had come, and it saddened her that Brutus could not tell her himself.

"Tell them," Brutus looked away from Portia, "tell them I will be there in a moment."

Chapter Six

C ALPURNIA watched as the priest blew on the flames rising from the altar. When the fire was bright and hot, the priest dropped the leg bones of an ox into the flames. The bones crackled and burst open, and the marrow hissed and sputtered as it oozed onto the burning coals.

"What does it say?" said Calpurnia, staring at the splinters of charred bone. She had woken up in the night when the lioness roared. Frightened, she had sent for the priest to ease her mind. "What do they tell you?!"

The priest reached his tongs into the fire and set the pieces of bone in a brass bowl to cool. He poked at them, studied them, then closed his eyes.

"What? What!?" shouted Calpurnia.

"The bones tell of some disaster," the priest said. "Caesar must stay far away from the Capitol tomorrow. Far away."

"Why?" said Calpurnia. "Speak!"

"I can read no more," said the priest, "but this much I know. Caesar must stay home."

Chapter Seven

"So it is settled," said Cassius. The men stood silently in Brutus' study. Outside, a gloomy dawn was turning into a gloomy morning. Nobody looked up as Cassius spoke. "Then let us here swear an oath."

"No oaths," said Brutus. "Oaths are for cowards, not brave men. If we believe what we are doing is right, then we need not swear an oath. If Caesar must die, as faithful Romans, we have no other choice but to kill him. Let our duty to Rome be our bond."

The men nodded, saying nothing. Finally Metellus spoke. "I'd still feel better if Cicero were part of this conspiracy."

"Conspiracy?" said Brutus. "This is not a conspiracy but a union of honest men with the courage to do what needs to be done."

"Right," said Metellus.

"Besides," said Casca, "Cicero is a politician. He will never go along with any idea unless he can claim it as his own."

Again there was silence.

"So," Decius cleared his throat, "are we to kill Caesar alone or should we get rid of his followers as well?"

"I think we should kill Marc Antony," said Cassius.

"We aren't going to *kill* anyone," said Brutus. "Our act will be sacrifice, not slaughter. Gentle friends, we may be bold but we are not wrathful. We are sacrificing Caesar for Rome."

Artemidorus, a kindhearted senator, looked away. He had joined the conspiracy because he believed in a democratic Rome, but all this talk was beginning to make him nervous.

"My fears are more practical," said Casca. "What if Caesar doesn't come to the Capitol? I have heard the old fool's wife has grown superstitious, and she fears the fortune-teller's warning to beware the Ides of March—which is today. What if she makes him stay home?"

"Leave that to me," said Decius. "I am to attend on him this morning. I will make sure he goes to the Capitol."

"Then that settles it," said Cassius quickly, suspecting that the courage of the conspirators would fade if they had any more time to think about their plan. "I am resolved. Casca?"

Casca paused. "Yes," he said. "If you are sure Caesar will come to the Capitol to be crowned today, I am resolved to stop it."

"Metellus?"

Metellus nodded. "Resolved."

"I am resolved," said Decius.

"Artemidorus?" said Cassius.

"Caesar shall not be king," said Artemidorus, still looking away.

Brutus took Cassius and Decius by the hands, and then all the men joined hands in a circle. "Good gentlemen," he said, "look fresh and merry. Let not our looks betray our intentions. By noon today, Rome shall be free once more."

Chapter Eight

"Help! Help! They murder Caesar! Caesar murdered! Help!" Caesar woke with a start. "Calpurnia!" He shook his wife. "Wake up. You are dreaming again."

Calpurnia opened her eyes and, upon seeing her husband's face, immediately smiled. "I dreamt they murdered you."

"For the third time tonight," said Caesar. "But it seems this night has all but passed." Caesar rose and opened the curtains onto the murky light of the morning.

"Don't go to the Capitol today, please," Calpurnia begged. "Last night a lioness gave birth in the streets and they say the dead walked out of their graves! Caesar, great Caesar, I don't like it. Don't go!"

"Why should I fear lions and dead men?" said Caesar. "Anything and anyone who looks on my face shrinks in terror. I have nothing to fear at the Capitol or anywhere else."

"Please, my lord. I never believed in superstitions, but they say—" Calpurnia broke off. It was too horrible to think about.

"What do they say?" said Caesar.

"Fierce fiery warriors fought upon the clouds and drizzled blood upon the Capitol. Oh, Caesar, these things are omens of some horrible violence. Please stay home today."

"Caesar cannot let these fearful wonders guide his actions," said Caesar, dressing. "Cowards die many times before their deaths. The valiant never taste of death but once. Of all the wonders that I yet have heard, it seems to me most strange that men should fear anything, given that we will all die at some point."

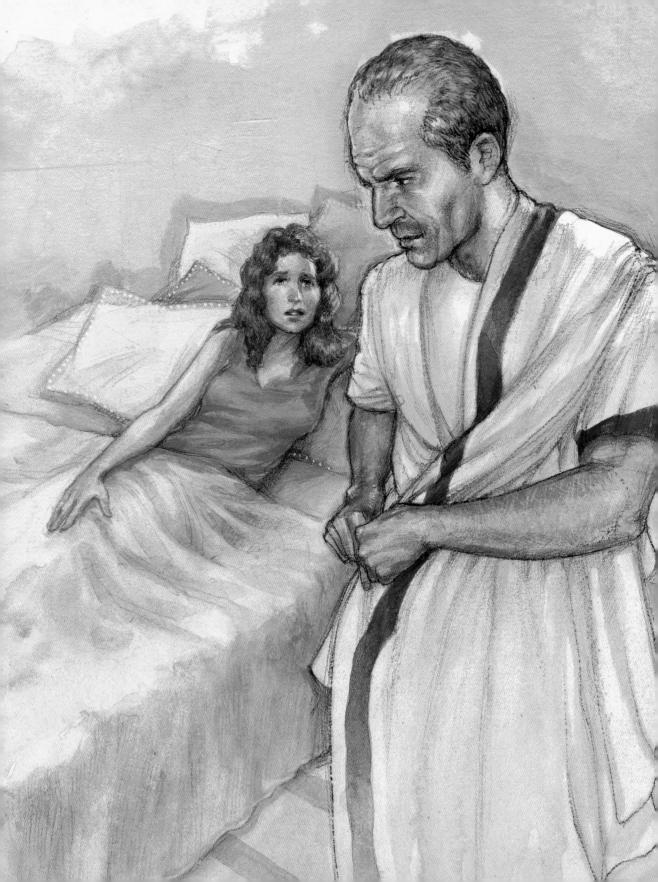

"But, my lord, I am frightened. Won't you please at least talk to the priest?"

"For you I will," said Caesar. "Send him in. We will have the strange events of last night explained."

Decius entered the room with a thin dark man in Egyptian clothing. "You called for a priest," said Decius.

"What do you make of these ghosts and fireballs that troubled us last night? Calpurnia wants to know."

The priest turned up his eyes as if he were trying to read words written on his brain. "You will be murdered in the Capitol today if you go. Stay home."

Decius went cold. Had Cassius' plan leaked out somehow?

"See, my lord?" said Calpurnia. "See? It is just as I dreamed!"

Caesar smiled, but he was obviously troubled. "Would staying home today make you happy, Calpurnia?"

"Yes, my lord. Please stay."

Decius thought quickly. The best way to get Caesar to do anything was to appeal to his vanity. "Good idea. We will send word that Caesar is ill, so the people will not know you were frightened of this strange prediction."

"I don't need to lie," said Caesar. "I am not coming to the Capitol because I am not coming. That's all anyone needs to know."

"But what shall I tell them when they ask me why?" said Decius.

"Tell them it is my will," said Caesar. "I need no other reason. But for you, Decius, I will tell you that I am not going because my wife had a dream."

"I saw my husband's statue stabbed a hundred times. I saw it spout blood, and I saw the Roman people bathe in it." Calpurnia trembled.

"Is this the cause of your fear?" said Decius. "Good Calpurnia, you have misinterpreted. This dream looks forward to the moment Caesar is king. The blood pouring forth from his statue signifies that life will be restored to this city, and the Romans bathing in Caesar's blood shows us how Caesar will rejuvenate us all. But if you want me to tell the Senate to put off crowning Caesar until his wife has happier dreams—"

"You will tell them no such thing," said Caesar. "Calpurnia, don't you see that your fears are misguided?"

"My lord, what day is it today?" she said.

"The fifteenth of March. Why do you ask?"

"The ides of March," she said. "The fortune-teller bid you to beware the ides of March. Now it is the ides of March. All these predictions agree! The omens, the warning, my dream. Oh, Caesar, my husband, I am frightened!"

Decius looked crossly at Calpurnia and then back to Caesar. "What shall I tell the senators?"

"Tell them Caesar comes."

Chapter Nine

"What time is it now?" said Portia to her servant. Brutus had left for the Senate not half an hour before, but it seemed like days. "Eight o'clock," he said.

"Go to the Senate," she said. "Tell me if there is any news."

"What news would there be?"

Portia could not tell a servant the news she was awaiting. "Just find my husband, Brutus," she snapped. "See if he is well. He did not look fit when he left."

The servant didn't ask any more questions. He had been a servant long enough to know that noble men and ladies had strange ways. There was no use arguing with them, but he did think gentlefolk would be better off doing more hard work and less thinking.

Portia went to the doorway and paced, studying the strange blue streaks of lightning that cut across the sky. *Something is wrong*, she thought. *If only I could be there by my husband's side!*

Just then the blind fortune-teller came down the street, tapping his stick along the cobblestones.

"You there!" said Portia. "Are you going to the Capitol?"

"Who's that? The gentle Portia?" he said. "Yes, I am going to the Capitol. To speak with Caesar. And if he is wise he will listen."

"Why? Do you know of some harm that will come to him?"

The fortune-teller cocked his head. "*Will* come? No. Nothing is for certain. Though it is very likely some harm will come to him if he doesn't listen to me. People can change their destiny, you know. Whether Caesar will or not remains to be seen. I hope so. He is a good man."

Portia watched the fortune-teller disappear down the street.

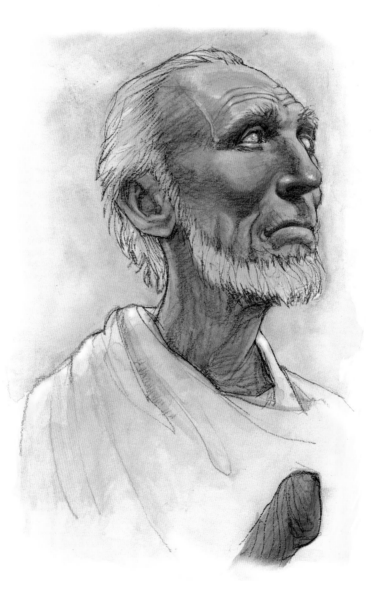

Chapter Ten

A RTEMIDORUS wrote quickly. If he weren't in place at the Senate soon the other conspirators would suspect he had betrayed them—and they would probably kill him. But he had to get word to Caesar. It was a chance he must take.

Conspirators. Artemidorus chewed on the word. They were conspirators. For all their talk of valor and saving Rome, they were no better than common criminals planning a murder. Artemidorus didn't want a king any more than anyone else. He might even go so far as to agree that Rome would be better off if Caesar were not around. But killing was killing. You might kill to defend yourself. You might kill to defend your city. But Caesar wasn't really threatening Rome, at least not as Artemidorus saw it. *Caesar, beware of Brutus,* he wrote. *Take heed of Cassius. Come not near Casca. Have an eye to Cinna. Trust not Trebonius, Metellus, or Decius. There is but one mind in these men, and it is bent against you.*

Caesar, he thought, *if you get this message before you get to the Capitol you may live. If not, then fate is on the side of the traitors.*

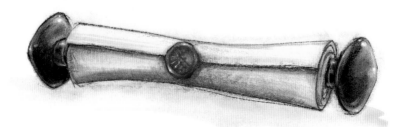

Chapter Eleven

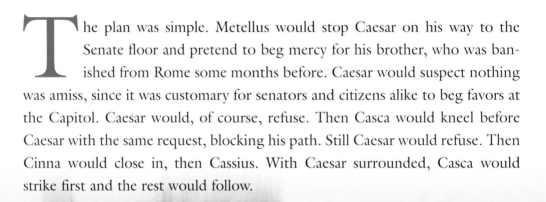

The plan was simple. Metellus would stop Caesar on his way to the Senate floor and pretend to beg mercy for his brother, who was banished from Rome some months before. Caesar would suspect nothing was amiss, since it was customary for senators and citizens alike to beg favors at the Capitol. Caesar would, of course, refuse. Then Casca would kneel before Caesar with the same request, blocking his path. Still Caesar would refuse. Then Cinna would close in, then Cassius. With Caesar surrounded, Casca would strike first and the rest would follow.

"Once the deed is done," said Brutus, "order will be restored."

"Yes," said Cassius, "but others will try to seize Rome once Caesar falls. Marc Antony will try. And he will call us murderers before we can show the people we are liberators."

"Cassius," said Brutus, "I know we will have Marc Antony as a friend when all is done. He is a noble Roman and so are we."

The door swung open and Trebonius stuck his head in. "Caesar comes," he said, his voice barely audible above the shouts and cries of thousands upon thousands of Romans who flocked to the Senate to welcome Caesar as their king.

"We are ready," said Brutus.

Cassius knew Brutus was wrong. The people would hate them for killing Caesar, at least for a while. If anyone provoked the people in those perilous moments after the murder, the city would explode. Marc Antony was clever enough to take advantage of this situation and ambitious enough to try. Brutus did not see this—or refused to see it—and that worried Cassius.

Chapter Twelve

CAESAR strutted up the hill to the Capitol, waving to the crowd. Poor men knelt at his feet begging for aid. Children waved ribbons. Women held their babies out for him to kiss. Citizens of all kinds ran to him, hoping he would hear their small complaints.

Caesar smiled at each, taking the time to stop and shake hands, if not to listen. Artemidorus stood beside Decius at the foot of the stairs leading to the Capitol. Here only the senators and other powerful men gathered, but they too wanted Caesar's ear.

Caesar marched on, his face painted with an expression of self-satisfaction.

"Caesar!" shouted Artemidorus, holding out a folded note "Read my petition!"

Petition? thought Decius. *That wasn't part of the plan.* What Artemidorus was up to he did not know, but he didn't like it. He jumped in front of Artemidorus' outstretched arm. "Listen to me, Caesar. Hear my complaint!"

Artemidorus pushed forward. "Caesar, read mine first. It concerns you personally."

Caesar stopped. "Then I will read it last." He took the note from Artemidorus and stuffed it into his robes. "What concerns me personally is not my concern. I am here for Rome."

Artemidorus grabbed Caesar's arm. "Read it now, Caesar. You must!"

"Is the man mad?" said Caesar.

Marc Antony gallantly pushed Artemidorus away.

Casca came up behind Artemidorus. "This business of yours is not part of our plan," he whispered.

Artemidorus pulled free of Casca. "I have no business with you," he said and ran.

Trebonius started after him.

"No," said Decius. "Leave him. We need you to distract Marc Antony."

Chapter Thirteen

Inside the Capitol there was an eerie calm. Caesar stepped to the center of the room as if the crowd still cheered him on, but only Brutus and Cassius were there. Decius, Casca, Cinna, and Metellus followed.

"A word with you, great Caesar, before we proceed to the Senate," said Brutus.

"Do you men have some petition for Caesar," said Caesar. "Where is Marc Antony?"

"Speaking with Trebonius," said Casca.

"Well, what is the trouble?" said Caesar.

Metellus approached. "Most high, most mighty, and most powerful Caesar, I throw myself before your greatness." He knelt.

"Get up!" roared Caesar. "These crouching courtesies might fire the blood of lowly men, but the blood of Caesar will not be thawed by fawning and sweet words."

"My brother is banished," Metellus went on. "Please—"

"Your brother is banished by law. If he, like you, imagines the rule of law should be swayed by this pathetic display then may he stay banished!"

"Pardon me, Caesar." Casca threw himself in front of Caesar's feet. "I beg you to reconsider."

"Will the senators of Rome lie like dogs on the floor?" said Caesar.

Brutus stepped forward. "If groveling is too humble, then let me kiss your hand and urge you to have mercy on Metellus' brother."

"I could be moved by this flattery," said Caesar directly to Brutus, "if I were like you. But I am not. There are many stars in the sky that turn and move as

the year passes, but there is one star—and one only—that holds its position while all the others turn around it. I am he—unshakable and motionless, constant and fixed as the northern star."

Now he thinks he's a star, thought Cassius. *I can't wait to kill him, the puffed up, arrogant fool.*

Cinna came beside Brutus. "Please, Caesar."

"You might as well try to lift Mount Olympus."

Decius went to Caesar's back. Brutus knelt. "Great Caesar, hear us."

"You are wasting your time kneeling," said Caesar.

"Then let my hands speak for me!" cried Casca, rising from the floor. His robes flying out like wings, he pulled his dagger from his belt and plunged it into Caesar's belly.

Decius sprung forward, twisting another blade into Caesar's back. Caesar coughed but did not fall. Cinna slashed Caesar across the chest. Cassius rushed forward and stabbed him in the neck.

Caesar fell to his knees, the blood pouring from his wounds. He was eye to eye with Brutus, still kneeling.

Brutus pulled his dagger out. Caesar stared at the gleaming blade in Brutus' hand—Brutus who had been his friend. Brutus lifted the dagger.

Blood bubbled from Caesar's mouth. "Et tu, Brute?" he said.

Brutus stuck the dagger through Caesar's heart.

Chapter Fourteen

There was silence in the Senate chamber. Caesar's blood flowed from him. The conspirators stood in the crimson pool, not certain what they had done.

Then Cinna laughed. "Ha! Ha ha!"

The others looked at him. "It is done!" Cinna cried. "Liberty! Freedom! Tyranny is dead! Run and proclaim it! Cry aloud in the streets."

Cassius, who had the foresight to guard the door, spoke quickly. "Hurry. We must go to the public squares and tell the people we did this to free them. We must lose no time!"

"Brutus should do it!" said Casca, agitated. "The people trust him. Brutus, you must do it at once!"

Decius had fallen to his knees. He was on the verge of madness, staring at the ruins of Caesar, fallen in his own blood. "What have we done?"

"What do you mean?" said Metellus. "We need to stay together now."

"Cassius, too," said Casca. "He should go and explain this to the people. It was his idea."

Cassius thought for a moment about killing Casca, but at that moment Trebonius slipped in through the door. He was pale.

"What's wrong?" said Cassius.

"Artemidorus betrayed us," he said. "Marc Antony knows and so does everyone else. Already the Roman people are in a frenzy. We are dead men."

They all looked at Brutus.

"We have nothing to fear," Brutus said. "Our reasons were just. Whether or not the Roman people agree is up to them."

Casca laughed bitterly. "If we are to trust the judgment of the Roman people then we really are dead men."

Cassius studied the men and was amazed at their weakness. They had wanted Caesar dead and now they had turned into helpless children. Now was the time to reason with the public, not to sit and wait for death. But he could not do it himself. He was a thinker, not a leader. He looked to Brutus.

Brutus stared at Caesar's body. "Remember, we are his friends," he said. His voice was far away. "We have preserved Rome." He dipped his fingers in the blood. "Let us bathe our hands in Caesar's blood—up to the elbows—and smear our swords with it. Then let us walk straight into the marketplace and wave our red weapons over our heads proudly and without shame. We will cry Peace! Freedom! and Liberty!"

"Yes," said Cassius. In truth, Cassius didn't think it wise to make the Roman people see the bloody truth of Caesar's death, but it was more important to keep the conspirators together, to show solidarity with Brutus, the man they now needed to lead them.

Cassius knelt beside Brutus cheerfully.

"Stoop, then, and wash. Many years from now, in cities still unborn and in accents yet unknown, they will remember and talk about what we did here today. Come, Romans, we shall walk out that door legends, not only for Rome but for all time. We shall be known as the men who gave their country liberty. Come and wash in Caesar's blood. Wear your honor proudly."

One by one the men knelt and scooped up the blood and rubbed it on their hands and arms.

"It will be great," Cassius said, as the silent and terrified men did as they were told. "We will be heroes. Brutus will lead us and we will be heroes."

At that moment Marc Antony pushed the door open and saw the men crouching like jackals around Caesar's body, covering themselves in his blood.

"O mighty Caesar!" Marc Antony said. "Do you now lie so low? Are all your conquests, glories, and triumphs shrunk to this?"

Chapter Fifteen

CASSIUS guarded the door to make sure Marc Antony couldn't leave, but now they had to decide what to do with him. "If you are going to kill me," said Marc Antony, "I would not die anywhere else but here beside Caesar and by no other sword than that which now drips with his blood!"

Brutus stood and held out his hands. "Do not fear us, Marc Antony. Although this deed appears cruel to you, our hearts are not. As bloody as our hands may be, we hold them open to receive you with love and brotherhood."

"You speak of brotherhood and love with bloody hands and daggers?"

"I will explain," said Brutus. "Just give us time to quiet the people first. I can tell you now, though, that we did this for Rome."

Cassius came behind Brutus. "Yes. And now that Rome is ours, do not think we will keep benefits from you, if you will cooperate."

Marc Antony could see that Brutus and Cassius had very different ideas about why Caesar was dead. Brutus spoke of duty while Cassius spoke of power. Clearly, there was disagreement in the heart of their deadly plan, disagreement that could be turned to his advantage. But for now he would play along. "Your word is as good as your honor, Brutus," said Marc Antony. "Come. Let each man give me his bloody hand. Brutus, Cassius, Decius, Metellus, Casca, Cinna. Come."

The men came forward to embrace Marc Antony. Brutus was last. "I am glad to count you a friend," he said.

"Yes." The stench of blood on Brutus' hands turned Marc Antony's stomach. "But I do ask one thing. Let me bear his body to the marketplace and give a funeral speech to the people."

"Of course, Marc Antony," said Brutus.

"A word with you, Brutus," said Cassius, pulling Brutus away by the arm. "It would be a great mistake to let Marc Antony talk to the people," he whispered. "He will turn them against us."

"Fear not," said Brutus. "I will speak first and show the people why Caesar had to die. As a show of faith I will tell them that I myself have urged Marc Antony to say some kind words over Caesar's body. The people will see we have nothing to hide."

"I don't like it," said Cassius. "The people don't think that clearly. They are not so reasonable. They feel and act on impulses, like beasts."

Brutus did not listen. Already he was imagining a bright new day for Rome that would begin with his triumphant speech in the city square. "Take the body to the marketplace, Marc Antony, and after I have spoken speak all the good you wish about Caesar. Only, you must tell the people that you speak by our permission. Will you follow these rules?"

"I ask no more," said Marc Antony. He shook hands again with the murderers as they made their way out of the Senate.

When the others had gone, Marc Antony looked down at the corpse of Caesar lying in a pool of blood. "Pardon me, you bleeding piece of earth, that I am meek and gentle with these butchers who left in ruins the noblest man that ever lived. Those who killed this man will pay for it, I will see to that. I will create domestic fury and civil strife. Blood and destruction will be so familiar by the time I am done that mothers will smile to see their children cut down. And Caesar's ghost will walk the earth and with the voice of a king cry 'Havoc!' and let loose the dogs of war!"

Chapter Sixteen

The marketplace buzzed with anticipation and confusion. Already the rumor had spread that Caesar had been killed in the Capitol, but another rumor followed quickly behind: that Caesar was not what he seemed. It was whispered that he had used people to advance his own ambitions. He had lied to them, and certain noble Romans had risked all to stop him. Or so it was said. The people didn't know what to think.

From out of the Capitol Brutus came, his arms bloody and his face serene. His eyes seemed to look out at the crowd and beyond it. He walked without fear. His confidence reassured the uneasy crowd. Calmly he climbed the steps to the base of a great statue of Pompey, a hero who had lived and died for the good of Rome and never asked to be king.

The people waited. Brutus raised his bloody hands. "Lovers of freedom," he said, "lovers of justice, and lovers of Rome. My friends and my countrymen, listen to what I have to say and judge me according to your wisdom."

"I rose against Caesar, it is true," continued Brutus, "not because I loved Caesar less, but because I loved Rome more."

"Brutus is nothing if not noble," said a man.

"But he murdered Caesar," said another. "Look at the blood on his hands!"

Brutus pointed to the man. "Let me ask you this: would you rather have Caesar alive and die slaves or have Caesar dead and live free men?"

The man hung his head in sadness and confusion.

"Believe me," said Brutus, "I loved Caesar, too. As he was my friend, I weep for him. As he was a hero, I rejoiced. As he was brave, I honored him. But as he wanted to lord over Rome, I killed him."

Lord over Rome. The phrase echoed in every ear. If Caesar was that ambitious, then perhaps he had to die.

"I know you have doubts," said Brutus, "but who here would want to be a slave? If there is any, speak, for I have offended him."

Nobody spoke.

"Who here values himself so little that he would not be a citizen of a free Rome? Speak, for I have offended him, too."

Again, nobody spoke.

"Who here does not love his country? Speak, for I have offended him."

This time somebody spoke. "Brutus is right!"

"Yes," shouted another. "Brutus did what he had to do!"

Brutus smiled. "I am glad I have offended no one. I am glad you all hold yourselves and Rome as dear as I do."

"Hooray for Brutus!" came a shout, and then the whole crowd followed. "Hooray! Hooray for Brutus!"

"But wait," said Brutus. "If there is any doubt that I did this deed for love of Rome then I make this promise." He pulled from his belt the same bloody dagger he plunged into Caesar's heart. "This is the blade that liberated Rome from a tyrant. With the same blade I will cut short my own life, if it pleases Rome. If you, the people of Rome, think I should die for what I have done, tell me and I will kill myself right here."

He touched the point of the dagger to his heart.

"Don't do it," came a voice.

"Long live Brutus!" came another. "Brutus saved us! Let Brutus be king!"

Brutus dropped his dagger. "Then I shall live—and may my life prove worthy of your wisdom and your confidence, my countrymen!"

Cheers rang out from every corner. But as Brutus stood admiring the work his words had done a hush slowly crept over the marketplace. Marc Antony had arrived. He carried Caesar's bleeding body.

Chapter Seventeen

"Romans," continued Brutus, "I ask you to refrain from celebrating this victory for just a moment." He was so caught up in his own moment of greatness he did not notice that the mood in the marketplace had changed. The people were staring at the broken body Marc Antony held in his arms, at the wounds that spoke more loudly than words to the violence that had been done. "Marc Antony has asked my permission to present a eulogy of Caesar, and I have granted it. I ask you to give him the same attention you would give me. Stay and listen while I return to the Capitol and put our city back in order."

Some applauded Brutus as he descended the stairs, but most were too astonished to say anything. There were so many wounds on the body.

"This is not good," said Cassius, who was lurking behind the statue of Pompey.

Casca nodded, absorbed in his own fears.

Marc Antony set Caesar's body down gently at the foot of the statue, as if it were a newborn baby. Heavy with grief, or seeming so, he faced the crowd.

"Friends. Romans. Countrymen. Lend me your ears," he began. "I come to bury Caesar not to praise him. The evil that men do lives after them, and the good is often buried with their bones. So let it be with Caesar."

"What evil deserved . . . *this?*" said one man, pointing to the body and turning his face away.

"What evil?" said Marc Antony. "Brutus has told you Caesar was ambitious, and such ambition comes with a price."

As Marc Antony spoke the words, the people gazed at Caesar's mangled body—thirty-three stab wounds in all. It was difficult for anyone to imagine a crime for which such brutality was a just punishment.

"But Caesar was my friend, despite his faults," Marc Antony went on, "and Brutus has given me permission to speak about the good that was in Caesar, since his faults have now been paid for. Caesar conquered distant lands and brought treasure home to share with us. These might not seem the actions of a tyrant, but Brutus said Caesar was ambitious, and Brutus is an honorable man."

"A man's not a tyrant just because he's ambitious!" someone yelled. "He conquered the world for us!"

Marc Antony held up his hand. "True. It did not seem like tyranny when Caesar risked his own life to make our city safer, but Brutus says Caesar was a tyrant, and Brutus, as you know, is an honorable man."

The crowd grew uneasy. A cry went up. "Honorable man? Where is the honor in this deed?"

"Look at all the wounds!" came a shriek.

Cassius whispered in Casca's ear. "We need to get out of here."

Casca was too frightened to respond.

"Peace, peace!" cried Marc Antony. "I, I cannot—" He broke off, pretending he was about to cry. "I am sorry. Be patient with me. I cannot help but weep that Caesar is dead, even though, as Brutus, honorable Brutus, says, he deserved it."

"He did nothing wrong!" cried a voice.

"Brutus is to blame!" came another.

"To think," said Marc Antony, "only yesterday the word of Caesar might have stood against the world. Now he lies there dead, mourned not even by the people of Rome whom he loved so dearly. I could show you . . . but no." He shook his head. "If I were to show you his will, you would see how much he loved you, but it would make you weep and hate the men who killed him."

"Read the will! Read the will!" shouted the crowd.

"No," said Marc Antony. "It would hurt too deeply."

"Read it! Read the will," they cried.

"If you insist, I will read it." Marc Antony withdrew a scroll from his robes.

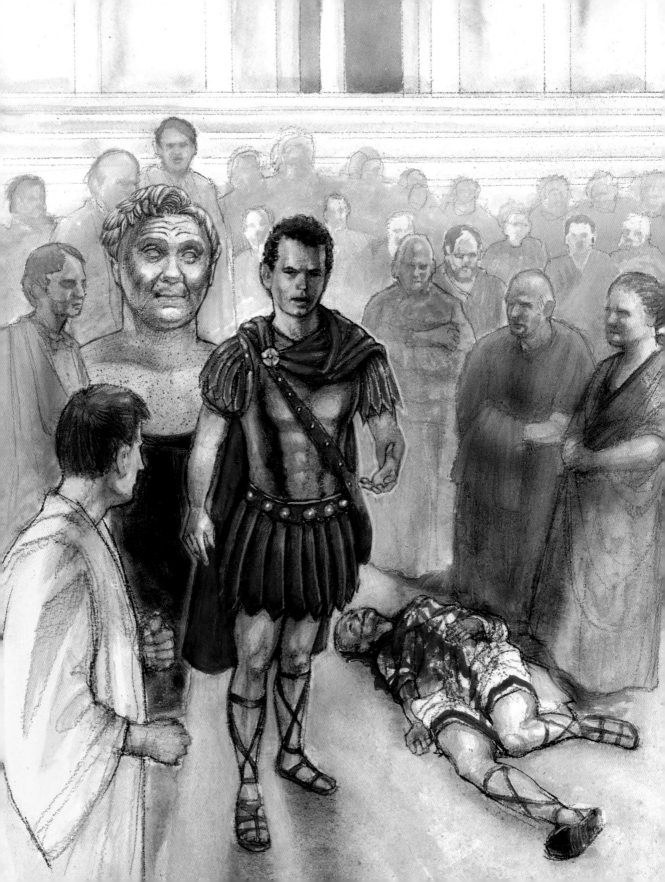

"Draw near and form a circle around Caesar's body."

As the crowd pressed forward Cassius grabbed Casca and hurried out of the marketplace.

"Caesar leaves to the Roman people all his houses and all his lands, to be turned into a public park—for you."

Silence.

"You are his heirs, his children," said Marc Antony. "He leaves all that was his to you and your families."

Marc Antony waited.

Finally, somebody spoke. It was the cobbler. "This deed was not done by honorable men. It was done by traitors."

"Not traitors, murderers," came another voice.

The crowd was now writhing with anger.

"He only wanted you to be happy," said Marc Antony. "All he did was for you. Perhaps they saw it differently—Cassius and Casca. Metellus. Cinna. Perhaps—"

"Kill them all!" the people cried. "Kill the traitors! Burn their houses!"

The crowd roared and heaved like a beast in a cage. Marc Antony did not try to calm it. "Maybe Brutus, whom Caesar loved most of all, had reasons for wanting to withhold Caesar's love and generosity from you."

"Kill him!" The people raised their fists in the air. "Kill Brutus! Burn Cassius in his house! Kill them! Kill them all!"

The people began to move. They turned from the statue and the bloody spectacle, revenge and hatred burning in their eyes. They stooped and grabbed rocks, boards, bricks—anything they could. "Kill them!" they cried. "Kill them all!"

When the crowd broke free, Marc Antony stood alone by the body of Caesar under the shadow of Pompey. He smiled. "Mischief is afoot. Now let it work."

Chapter Eighteen

From a cottage that overlooked a bend in the Tiber, in a quiet part of town where people came on holidays to feed the geese and watch artists paint, a poet, who shared the name of Cinna, opened his door. He had been up late writing and had slept little.

He had dreamt of Caesar, which was strange since he did not follow politics. He liked Caesar well enough, but felt that one ruler was more or less like any other. Books were more important to him than governments. Books were eternal. Governments passed away and were quickly forgotten.

In his dream he sat at Caesar's table, listening to the senators and generals argue about their wars and their policies and their schemes. He sat there as the great men of Rome talked without listening. He wondered why he was there at all.

And when he awoke from his dream he learned of Caesar's death.

Had it been a premonition? If so, why had it come to him, a poor poet who cared nothing for politics? He tried to push the dream out of his head by reading, but it was no use. The voices filled his ears, as the memory of dreams will. He did not want to leave his house, but he did not want to be alone either.

He thought he would go down to the marketplace where it was said there would be a funeral for Caesar. If paying respects to the body would not make the voices stop, at least it would be nice to get some fresh air and see other people.

On his way he heard a sound like a wave roaring down the cobblestone street. Within moments he found himself in a sea of angry men, men with torches and clubs and bricks. They surrounded him.

"Who are you?" one man said.

"What are you doing here?" said another.

"I live here," said Cinna. "That's my house, such as it is." He pointed to his humble cottage.

"Are you married?" asked one man.

"No," said Cinna, "I live alone. But I guess you would say I am married to my work. I'm a poet."

"So folks who are married are not as smart as you, is that what you're say-ing, poet?" A scar-faced man with no front teeth jabbed Cinna in the ribs with a board.

"No," Cinna insisted. "No. Please, don't hurt me. I was only trying to answer your question."

"You answer with too many words, but poets are always thinking and writ-ing too much while other men are working," said another man. "If you're so smart, what do you think of Caesar's death?"

"I think it is sad when any man dies," said Cinna. "I was going down to his funeral."

"As a friend?"

"As a Roman," said Cinna.

"That's not an answer," said the scar-faced man. "Whose side are you on?"

"Side? Aren't we all on the same side?" said Cinna.

"Are you telling us you don't know there was a conspiracy to kill Caesar?" the man said.

"You'd better tell us who are you," said another voice.

"A Roman," said Cinna, "like you."

"We'll be the judge of that," said a man. "Your name!"

"My name is Cinna."

The mob twitched with rage and hatred. "Cinna was one of them that killed Caesar!" came a voice. "He's a conspirator!"

"Kill him!"

A rock smashed Cinna in the face. "Ahhh! No! You have the wrong man. I killed no one. I am Cinna the poet, not Cinna the conspirator!"

"Then kill him for his bad poetry!"

"Tear him to pieces."

"Please!" Cinna begged.

But it was too late. He felt the breath of the men as they closed in. Then he felt their clubs and the fire of their torches.

Then he felt nothing.

Chapter Nineteen

MARC ANTONY, moving quickly to gain control of Rome, had called a meeting with two generals whose legions were encamped outside the city. One was Octavius, a brash and talented young officer with limitless energy and a taste for power, which he gained and wielded with ruthless efficiency. Marc Antony feared Octavius but knew he would be a powerful ally against Brutus. The other general was Lepidus. Marc Antony regarded him as a faithful soldier but a simpleton with whom he did not want to share power in Rome. Octavius had insisted that Lepidus' forces would be needed in the fight against Brutus, but Marc Antony mistrusted Octavius' motives.

"So who else must be eliminated?" said Octavius.

"Publius," said Marc Antony. "Lepidus' brother."

Lepidus folded his hands and frowned.

"Lepidus, your brother is an enemy of the new order," said Octavius. "He needs to be killed. Do you object?" Octavius stared at Lepidus and tapped the table with his pen.

"No," Lepidus said, pushing his chair back and standing. "I object to nothing." He went to the door. "I will be at Caesar's house going over the will."

"We will join you," said Marc Antony.

Lepidus left.

"This is a slight and pathetic man," Marc Antony said. "Good for nothing but running errands."

"He has proven himself on the battlefield," said Octavius.

"So has my horse," said Marc Antony, "and for that I give him oats. Why are we dividing up Rome with him?"

"Brutus will fight bitterly. If our fight against him does not go well, we will need to draw on Lepidus and his men."

"You will see," said Marc Antony, "when you have experienced as much of politics as I have. Winning a battle is easy. Maintaining power is the hard part. Lepidus may help us defeat Brutus, but you won't be so happy when later he proves himself too weak and too stupid to do anything but follow your orders."

"Then he will follow my orders," said Octavius, leaning back in his chair and glaring somewhat defiantly at Marc Antony. "Or should I say *our* orders."

Octavius is dangerous, thought Marc Antony, *but politics are dangerous. Use him to destroy Brutus now and deal with him later.* "My emotions got the better of me," he said. "Let's talk no more of Lepidus. What do we know about Brutus?"

Octavius unrolled a map. "Brutus has fled the city. Cassius, Metellus, and Casca as well. As for the other conspirators, they are dead. Now, Brutus has encamped his forces here." Octavius pointed to a hilltop. "Cassius has brought his army to the river side. My spies tell me there is unrest between the two rebels. If we move our forces south . . ."

As Octavius spoke, Marc Antony watched the young man's finger moving across the map of Rome. Glorious and eternal Rome. The greatest power the world had ever known. His. It was all his.

Chapter Twenty

RUTUS looked down across the plain at the campfires of Mark Antony's forces. His moment of greatness had been all too brief. No sooner had he returned to his home than the streets of Rome erupted in violence. It was a level of hatred he had not thought possible from citizens he considered the most civilized in all the world. They came with sticks and torches, hammers and scythes, spite and malice. Citizens he had served his whole life had forced him to flee his own city.

Brutus escaped the city with a small band of soldiers, who Cassius said were loyal to the Republic. But their loyalty had proven only as deep as Brutus' purse. With money running out, the soldiers grew restless. Many had fled and Cassius would provide no more money.

Men are hollow, thought Brutus as he watched Cassius marching up the hill, haughty and defiant. *They snort like stallions on parade, but put a spur to them and they hang their heads like a farmer's nag.*

"Brutus!" said Cassius, tearing his helmet off. "Is it true that you believe I have withheld money from our cause? You have done me wrong!"

"You have done yourself wrong, old friend," said Brutus, "to keep your gold when we need it to pay the soldiers."

Cassius stepped closer. "If it were anyone but you who said this I would kill him."

Brutus pushed passed Cassius and stared once more at the campfires. "Tell me, Cassius, did Caesar die for the sake of justice or money? Have we now proven ourselves no better than the enemies of democracy who wanted to make him king?"

Cassius squared in front of Brutus. "Don't bait me," he said. "You forget whom you are talking to!"

"You forget the man you were," said Brutus. "Go. You are not the Cassius I knew."

"You put too much trust in our friendship. I would kill any man who insulted me like that."

"I *have* put too much trust in our friendship," said Brutus. "And if you would kill me to defend your honor it would please me, for then I would know you still have honor."

Cassius had held back the money, it was true, but not out of greed. The war—if it could be won at all—would be long and costly, and the money had to last. Brutus did not understand this—or any of the other hard realities of maintaining power.

"If you believe I am without honor," said Cassius, pulling out his dagger and handing it to Brutus, "then kill me right here."

"There is no need," said Brutus. "All is lost."

"Make way, make way!" Just then, Casca and Metellus appeared at the top of the hill. "Generals," said Metellus, "Octavius and Marc Antony have put a hundred senators to death, old Cicero among them."

"Cicero," said Brutus. "I wouldn't have thought they would stoop so low."

"They have stooped even lower," said Casca. He put his hand on Brutus' shoulder. "Your wife Portia is dead. The manner of death was . . . unusual."

Brutus listened to the news. There was no beauty left in the world, no goodness. Of course someone as beautiful and perfect as Portia could not live in a world that had become so bad. "Then we must attack now," he said, "for there is nothing left to lose."

Cassius saw the hopelessness in Brutus, and it worried him. To attack now was certain death. Perhaps that is what Brutus wanted.

"We should wait," said Cassius.

"Why?" said Brutus. "Every day the enemy grows mightier. Our numbers dwindle. We shall never be stronger than we are at this moment."

"I agree with Cassius," said Casca. "We should wait."

"Then we shall wait," said Brutus. He was tired and didn't have anything left to say.

Cassius departed with Casca and Metellus, leaving Brutus to himself.

He drank some water. It tasted like nothing on his tongue. The world was gone. There was nothing to do but wait for death. He went to his tent. There he found something he did not expect.

It was Caesar.

"What are you?!" said Brutus, the fear suddenly jolting him back into the world.

"Your evil spirit, Brutus," the figure said.

"Why did you come?"

"To tell you I will see you in the battle."

Brutus felt the world fade away again as he stared transfixed at the gaping black wounds upon the apparition's body and the hollow pits that were its eyes. It had a stink of death to it and it sounded like death, if death had a sound. But the more he watched it the less real the world became and the more real the figure seemed.

"So I will see you again?" Brutus said, as if he were speaking to Portia before leaving his house on an ordinary day.

"Yes." The ghost laughed. "On the battlefield."

It vanished.

Alone, Brutus sat on his bed. He thought once more about Portia. He was glad she had not lived to see his ruin.

Then he rose and donned his armor. There was no point in waiting. If everything were going to end, it might as well be now.

Chapter Twenty-One

BRUTUS rode high in the saddle, with two horsemen behind him holding his banners aloft in the light of dawn. He inhaled deeply the cool Roman air. His despair had been replaced by a calming sense of pride. It had been his greatest privilege to live in Rome, and there was no other place where he wanted to die.

Cassius rode beside him. His mind was less on the softness of the morning than on the positions of the enemy forces. There was a chance—although a small one—that they could win the battle. They would have to attack and withdraw perfectly, striking when the enemy was least prepared and regaining their position on the top of the hill. And they would need some luck.

"Sound a salute," said Brutus, and a bugler blew a high clear note.

It was hardly necessary. The forces of Marc Antony and Octavius were already lined up, flanking their two great generals.

"Ready the charge!" shouted Octavius.

"Hold. Let them have their say," said Marc Antony. "Because I have a few words for Brutus."

"Words?" said Octavius. "His forces are in the open. Now is our chance."

"Why do you cross me?" said Marc Antony.

"I'm not crossing you. You may do whatever you will," said Octavius, "but I'm going to attack him. Ready the charge!" he shouted again.

Marc Antony rode forward before Octavius gave the order, his banners lowered as a gesture of peace.

Octavius thought for a moment about charging anyway, right over Marc Antony's back, but he ordered his men to hold.

"So you will talk before we exchange death?" shouted Brutus. "That is very Roman of you."

"This from a man who said 'Peace, liberty, and freedom!' while cutting a hole in Caesar's heart," scoffed Marc Antony.

"And your sweet words transformed the streets of Rome into a slaughter-house," said Cassius. *If only I had been in charge and not Brutus*, he thought. *Marc Antony would never have turned the mob against us. Indeed, he never would have spoken again.*

Octavius drew his sword. "Enough talk. Now is the time for traitors to die."

"Put your sword away, young man," said Brutus. "There are no traitors here unless you are one."

"You waste your time talking to this schoolboy, Brutus," said Cassius, hoping to provoke a battle before the enemy was fully prepared.

"I have heard enough," said Octavius. "Come, Marc Antony. If they want to talk, they can try to do so while I am marching over them." He turned his horse and rode back to the line.

Marc Antony followed.

"Marc Antony is still a coward, look!" said Cassius. "Octavius is hot for war, but the fat old fool wants no part of it. Let's withdraw and let them come on. Watch! Octavius will charge us by himself while Antony sharpens his tongue and eats his cakes. Octavius' forces alone will break against our defenses, and then we can swoop down and destroy Marc Antony."

Brutus just watched the horses glide through the morning air, the banners streaming behind them. "If we fight this fight, we will surely die," he said.

"What?" said Cassius. His old friend was drifting away again. He had to refocus his mind on the work at hand. "So you will let them take you captive?"

"No," said Brutus. "I will not go in shackles back to Rome. This day must end what the ides of March began." He smiled. "If we do meet again, when this is over, it shall be a happy day. If not, then I am happy now to say goodbye."

Cassius was not so certain he was going to die, but the important thing now was to make sure Brutus was prepared to fight. "Yes," he said, "if this is our last act together, it will be a noble one! Come, let's get back up the hill and ready ourselves for what is to come."

Cassius rode on. Brutus followed. They were halfway up the hill when Brutus turned his horse around.

Cassius knew what Brutus was about to do. "No!" he cried.

Brutus raised his sword. *Now is the time*, he thought. *Now is the time to end the waiting.*

"Brutus," Cassius pleaded. "No."

But it was too late. "Ride! Ride!" Brutus shouted, spurring his horse. "Ride! For liberty, for freedom, and for Rome!"

Chapter Twenty-Two

CASSIUS shouted orders through the dust, trying to maintain order among his own men as Brutus' horsemen whirled around them. "Are we charging down there on the open field?!" said Casca, confused and only half dressed.

"We are now," said Cassius. "Look out!"

Cassius pulled Casca out of the way of the rushing horsemen.

"Should we sound the charge, my lord?!" said Cassius' lieutenant.

"No . . . I mean . . . wait. Just wait!"

On the plain below, the clash of metal rang out. Men shouted. Horses brayed. Arrows flew in.

Cassius spat a curse. "Brutus has attacked too soon!"

"What should we do?!" asked Casca.

The lieutenant looked at Cassius with wide eyes. Already his men, uncertain of what was happening, were rushing to join the battle. Others were running away.

"Follow me," said Cassius. "We'll try to get around the flank. It's our only hope. Sound the charge!"

Cassius whirled his horse around and flew off, trying to lead his forces to the weak side of the enemy's line but knowing it was almost hopeless. Brutus had sealed their doom.

Looks like you'll die today, Brutus, just as you wanted, thought Cassius, as he drove his horse through a storm of arrows.

"This is better than I could have hoped," said Marc Antony from his spot in a stand of trees, where he held his own forces safely in reserve. "The traitors are in disarray. Octavius cuts through the terrified fools like a young Mars. We will win this battle without a scratch."

"My lord," said his lieutenant. "Look there. Quickly!"

The enemy was breaking through Octavius' weak flank. If the line broke . . . "My lord!" The lieutenant was shouting now. "It's Cassius! He has outflanked Octavius. Soon he will be on us."

Marc Antony felt the sweat bead under his armor. "Are the men ready to fight?"

"They will have no choice," said the lieutenant.

The first arrow struck a tree beside them. Marc Antony ducked behind his horse's head. Then the crash came as the full force of Cassius' men drove like a wedge into Octavius' exposed flank.

"Charge behind Octavius' power," said Marc Antony. "Let the weak flank fall. We will march through the routed Brutus' men and up to the hill. Forget about the weak flank. It is lost!"

Cassius struck at the heads of the foot soldiers from his horse. He had received a sword stroke below the knee and could no longer feel his foot, if it was there. He dared not look down. It was a wound he would not survive. There was nothing to do but fight on now until his strength failed.

"Cassius," said Casca, "look! The camp burns!"

Smoke rose from the top of the hill where Cassius had hoped to win a defensive battle. Marc Antony's men swarmed up the hill like ants, stepping over the ruins of Brutus' army.

An arrow struck Cassius in the shoulder. He was already too numb to feel it.

"Cassius!" yelled Casca, riding to Cassius and trying to hold his body up.

The flames of the burning camp filled Cassius' dying eyes. In that moment, with the end so near, simple thoughts filled his mind. Simple innocent thoughts that pushed away all the hunger and the want and the envy that had consumed him. He thought about Rome in springtime. The geese on the river. The white stone of the Senate. Brutus and all his beautifully naive ideas. Portia loving Brutus for them. And Caesar. Old strutting Caesar, deaf and comical, but great in his own way. Rome was happy then.

"There is a dagger in my belt," Cassius whispered. "The same that killed Caesar."

Casca knew what his friend was about to ask.

"It is just that I should die on it." Cassius closed his eyes. "I want to die justly." He was murmuring now. "Let me die justly, my friend."

Casca held Cassius in his arms. He felt the tears and blood roll soft and warm down his chest. "I know," said Casca. "I want to die justly, too."

He plunged the dagger into Cassius' heart and then, with the blade wet with Cassius' blood, into his own.

Chapter Twenty-Three

❦

Dazed and weary, Brutus stumbled through the chaos. The battle was all but over. Those who could, fled. Those who could not, lay waiting for death. Horses writhed and snorted on the smoking earth. Arrows and broken spears stuck in the ground like black flowers growing in the land of death.

On the ground beside a dead horse Brutus saw Casca holding Cassius in one arm and a dagger in the other.

"These are the last of the true Romans. I owe more tears to them than I can pay." Brutus knelt and touched Cassius' face. "But I shall find time, Cassius. I shall find the time."

"They were cold-blooded killers who used your love of Rome to serve their own lust for power," came a voice.

Brutus hoped it was Caesar's ghost, come to strike him down. That way he could die next to his friends and look no more on the destruction he had caused. But it was not Caesar. It was Artemidorus, who had fought on Marc Antony's side. Even Caesar's ghost had failed him.

"But they are dead now," said Artemidorus, "and I have killed Metellus myself. Their crimes are repaid. As for you, Brutus, I always thought you noble, and although I cannot forgive you I will spare you. Go. Make what life you can."

Brutus wasn't listening. He was looking at the faces of Cassius and Casca. They were serene. At peace. Happy even. He thought about the battle he had just walked through without so much as a bruise. Now, as a reward for his good

fortune, he had to endure the memory of all that had happened and the dread for what was to come.

"Brutus," said Artemidorus, "you don't have time to wait here. Go now. Think about your crimes and live honestly. But go."

"No," Brutus said, "my hour has come."

A horn sounded. It was Octavius and Marc Antony, riding on with their victorious forces.

"There are your new kings," said Brutus. "I could not save Rome from them after all."

Artemidorus watched the two generals. Their proud faces shone with triumph and glee. And something else. Power. They rode like men who knew the world and everything in it was theirs and theirs alone.

"You are an honorable man, Artemidorus," said Brutus. "May you live long and enjoy your life in whatever may be left of Rome when all this is over. But I ask you to spare me from that future. I can endure my own pain, but I cannot watch Rome wither under the weight of kings."

Here is a noble Roman, Artemidorus thought.

"Hold out your sword," said Brutus.

Artemidorus knew what Brutus meant. "Give me your hand first," he said. The two men clasped hands. Artemidorus withdrew his sword.

"Farewell," said Brutus.

Brutus released Artemidorus' hand, took a deep breath, and then ran himself through on the outstretched blade.

Brutus fell.

"Good-bye, old friend," said Artemidorus.

"Is that Brutus?" said Marc Antony, dismounting and coming forward.

"It is," said Artemidorus. "Dead."

A crowd of soldiers gathered around the body. Brutus had been strong to the end, and the men who gazed down on him were moved with pity and admiration. Some began to murmur about the passion and conviction that had guided his life and the courage that had brought him to death.

Marc Antony stepped to the body and raised his hands, as he had done once before in the market square. "This," he said when the murmuring ceased, "was the noblest Roman of them all. Of the conspirators only he was honest and thought purely of the common good. His life was gentle. Everything about him declared to all the world that this was a true man!"

The soldiers crowded around Marc Antony. He seemed as if he were about to say more when Octavius pushed his way past him to Brutus' body.

"Lift up his bones," said Octavius. "He was valiant and will rest tonight like a true soldier, in my tent. Carry him through this field of victory with all the honor he deserves!"

The soldiers looked at Octavius and at Marc Antony, not sure which was in charge but not really caring either. The fighting was over. Nothing else mattered now. They lifted Brutus on their shoulders and bore his weight gently through the ranks of the silent dead.

JULIUS CAESAR

Is the Roman Republic different from the Roman Empire?

A republic is a state governed by the consent of the people. An empire is a vast and often diverse territory governed by a single power, usually a king or emperor. When we say "Rome" we think "Roman Empire" and imagine a territory consisting of almost all of Western Europe and the lands bordering the Mediterranean Sea. In truth, a great civilization was established in Rome long before Rome became an empire. Around 509 B.C. Rome was formed as a republic governed by representatives of the territory's different tribes and social groups. Rome began to conquer territory aggressively about three hundred years later. Julius Caesar was the greatest of the Roman conquerors, claiming what is now France and England in the first century B.C. Although Rome was then still a republic, Julius Caesar ruled it as dictator. After his death and up until the time of the collapse of Rome some five-hundred years later, Rome would be ruled by emperors who called themselves "Caesars" in honor of the man who turned Rome into an imperial power (the modern German and Russian words for "king"—*kaiser* and *czar*—come from this tradition).

Who or what are "tribunes"?

While Rome was still a republic, the tribunes were government officials elected or appointed by the general population. Their job was not only to represent ordinary people in government but also to protect them from injustice or abuse at the hands of wealthier and more powerful citizens. They were supposed to be available to the people twenty-four hours a day, seven days a week, and, by law, they were protected from any physical harm.

What is a "Colossus"?

The Colossus of Rhodes is a legendary statue that was supposed to be so large its feet could span the mouth of the harbor at Rhodes—an island near Greece. It is one of the so-called "Seven Wonders of the Ancient World." The others are the Hanging Gardens of Babylon, the Lighthouse of Alexandria, the Mausoleum of Halicarnassus, the seated statue of Zeus at Olympia, the Temple of Artemis at Ephesus, and the Great Pyramid in Egypt. Most of the Seven Wonders were destroyed and are known to us only through exaggerated reports. How large the Colossus actually was and where it stood in the harbor at Rhodes is anyone's guess.

What is the "Tiber"?

The Tiber is the river that flows through Rome. Like the Thames in London and the Seine in Paris, it is not one of the principal rivers of the world, but has become legendary due to the importance of the city built upon it.

What is the "ides of March"?

"Ides" is a term we no longer use, except in reference to *Julius Caesar*. In the old Roman calendar, the "ides" was merely the fifteenth or thirteenth day, whichever was the midpoint of the month.

Who or what are the Fates?

In Greek and Roman mythology, the Fates were three sisters who determined when human beings would die. Their names were Clotho, Lachesis, and Atropos. According to legend, Clotho would spin the yarn of each person's life, Lachesis would measure it, and Atropos would cut it.

Why does Julius Caesar refer to himself as the "Northern Star"?

Polaris is called the Northern Star or the Pole Star because its location in the heavens is directly over the North Pole and thus, as viewed from Earth, it appears to stand still while the other stars orbit around it.

WHO'S WHO IN
JULIUS CAESAR

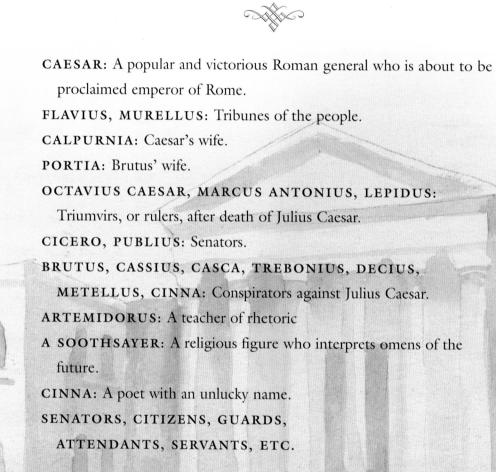

CAESAR: A popular and victorious Roman general who is about to be proclaimed emperor of Rome.

FLAVIUS, MURELLUS: Tribunes of the people.

CALPURNIA: Caesar's wife.

PORTIA: Brutus' wife.

OCTAVIUS CAESAR, MARCUS ANTONIUS, LEPIDUS: Triumvirs, or rulers, after death of Julius Caesar.

CICERO, PUBLIUS: Senators.

BRUTUS, CASSIUS, CASCA, TREBONIUS, DECIUS, METELLUS, CINNA: Conspirators against Julius Caesar.

ARTEMIDORUS: A teacher of rhetoric

A SOOTHSAYER: A religious figure who interprets omens of the future.

CINNA: A poet with an unlucky name.

SENATORS, CITIZENS, GUARDS, ATTENDANTS, SERVANTS, ETC.

INDEX